To Jeremy Eugene Orgel, a good and knowing doctor
—D. O.

To my family back home
—A. B.

Reteller's Note

When I was little my mother gave me her childhood book of tales from Grimm (in German, our language then). I'd shut my eyes and let it fall open to whichever tale it wanted me to read. But I'd only want to read it if it had a kid in it. And "Doctor All-Knowing" didn't!

Well, now it does. I turned the doctor's wife into a little daughter. Up in Retellers' Heaven, the Brothers Grimm approve, I think. Why would they mind? They know retellers switch things around a bit. They did it too, quite freely. I hope they welcome Maggie to their fulfilling, fun-filled story.

I owe thanks to Richard Jackson for lending it his rich imagination; and to Alexandra Boiger for bringing it glowingly alive.

—Doris Orgel

Atheneum Books for Young Readers
An imprint of Simon & Schuster Children's Publishing Division
1230 Avenue of the Americas, New York, New York 10020
Text copyright © 2008 by Doris Orgel
Illustrations copyright © 2008 by Alexandra Boiger
Book design by Ann Bobco
The text for this book is set in Book Antiqua.
The illustrations for this book are rendered in watercolor.
Manufactured in China
First Edition
10 9 8 7 6 5 4 3 2 1
Library of Congress Cataloging-in-Publication Data
Orgel, Doris.
Doctor All-Knowing : a folk tale from the brothers Grimm / retold by Doris Orgel ; illustrated by Alexandra Boiger. — 1st ed.
p.   cm.
"A Richard Jackson Book."
Summary: Desperate to provide enough food for himself and his daughter, a poor man sets himself up as Doctor All-Knowing and is soon called upon by a rich man to find a thief.
ISBN-13: 978-1-4169-1246-0
ISBN-10: 1-4169-1246-0
[1. Folklore—Germany.] I. Boiger, Alexandra, ill. II. Grimm, Jacob, 1785–1863. III. Grimm, Wilhelm, 1786–1859. IV. Doctor Know-All. English. V. Title.
PZ8.1.O59Doc 2008
398.2—dc22 [E]
2006023614

Doctor All-Knowing

$\mathscr{A}$ Folk Tale from the Brothers Grimm

Retold by Doris Orgel

Illustrated by Alexandra Boiger

A Richard Jackson Book Atheneum Books for Young Readers New York London Toronto Sydney

Long ago there lived a peasant named Crayfish and his little daughter, Maggie. They were very poor. All they ever had for supper was watery porridge. Nothing more. No second course. No third. No fourth. And never any cake, or pie, or pudding for dessert.

"Maggie, my dear good child, I wish I could give you meals with many delicious courses," her father often said.

One day poor Crayfish drove his oxcart into town and delivered a load of wood to a doctor. And Maggie came too. The doctor was a well-fed man, and rich.

"I'll pay for the wood when I've eaten," he said, and sat down to his midday meal. Crayfish and Maggie stood and waited. They watched him slurping sweet-potato soup. That was the first course of the meal.

Next he ate the second course, dandelion salad, then the third course, rainbow trout, then the fourth course, roasted duck. Finally he downed a slice of chocolate-cherry cake with a dollop of whipped cream on top.

Poor, hungry Maggie—she had such misery and longing in her eyes!

Crayfish gathered up his courage and asked the rich, round-bellied man, "Sir, could *I* become a doctor too?"

"Yes, easily," the doctor said.

"What must I do?"

"First, buy a doctoring book."

"But, Sir, I don't know how to read—"

"Well, then get an ABC book, one with a rooster in it. Second, sell your ox and cart and buy yourself a proper suit—one with a vest, the kind we doctors wear. Third, get a sign that says 'Doctor All-Knowing' and nail it above your door."

The doctor cut himself another slice of cake and ate every crumb of it. Then at last he paid—but only fifteen pennies!—for the wood.

Crayfish bought an ABC book that had a rooster in it. He sold his ox and cart, but for less money than what he had to spend to buy the doctor suit and sign. So now he was even poorer. And he started doctoring.

Not far away, in a palatial mansion, lived a man far richer than the round-bellied doctor. But, to his anger and dismay, much of his money'd been stolen—a fortune, if truth be told.

When he heard that a "Doctor All-Knowing" was doctoring nearby, he thought, *All-knowing? Good, he'll know who stole my money, and show me where it is.*

The rich man rode off in his elegant coach to the hut with the sign above the door. He knocked, and asked Crayfish, "Are you Doctor All-Knowing?"

"Yes, I am."

"Then will you kindly come and help me get back money that thieves stole from me?"

"Yes, I will. But my little daughter, Maggie, must come too."

"Very well." The rich man invited them into his coach. And off they rode to his palatial mansion.

They went in.

The rich man asked, "Doctor All-Knowing, will you dine with me?"

"Yes, I will. But Maggie must dine too."

"Very well."

They sat down at the table.

A servant came in with a soup tureen. Crayfish nudged Maggie and whispered, "That's the first . . . ," meaning the first course of the meal.

But the servant got scared. He thought the doctor meant, That's the first *thief*—which he, the servant, happened to be. He rushed into the kitchen and told the others, "Friends, we're done for. That doctor *knows*! He's on to us—he said I was the first!"

The second servant didn't want to carry in the second course, the salad.

But he had to. Then he, too, got scared when the doctor nudged his daughter,

saying, "Maggie, that's the second . . . "

The third servant carried in course number three, leg of lamb, and trembled with fear when the doctor nudged Maggie, saying, "There, child, that's the third . . ."

The fourth servant brought
in a dish with a silver cover over
it. And the rich man said, "Doctor,
now prove you're all-knowing. Tell me
what's under that cover."

The poor peasant sighed. He was stumped.
He had no idea. *What could it be?* he wondered,
and groaned, "Ah me, poor Crayfish!"

The fourth servant lifted the cover. And what do
you think lay on the dish?

Three large crayfish, pink and buttery.

"Amazing! You *are* all-knowing!" exclaimed the rich man.

"You must know who stole my money. Tell me!"

The fourth servant heard this, and got so scared, he shivered in his shoes. He sent the doctor frantic looks and pointed to the door, imploring, *Follow me!*

Crayfish stood up.

"No, Papa, stay!" Maggie didn't want to sit there without him.

"Don't worry, I'll be back soon. Meanwhile, look at the pictures in this book." He handed the ABC book to her. "See if you can find the rooster." Then he followed the fourth servant into the kitchen.

When they saw the all-knowing doctor come in, the four servants and the cook said, "We confess! We're the thieves. But we'll show you where we hid the money, and we'll give you some as your reward—" They got down on their knees and begged, "Oh, please don't tell the master, or he'll hang us!"

Then they led him out the kitchen door,

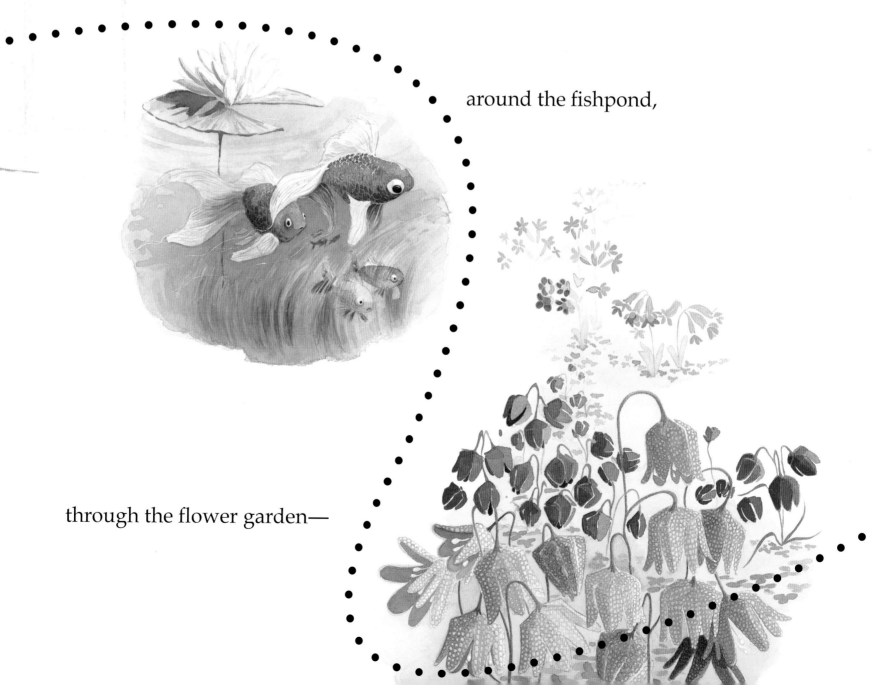

around the fishpond,

through the flower garden—

—and to the chicken coop.

A rooster stood on it and crowed,

"Kee-ker-ree-kee-kee!"

Aha, thought Crayfish, *now I know!*

They returned to the house, and the thieves

kept begging, "Doctor, don't betray us!"

Maggie was glad when he came in and sat down beside her.

"But Papa, I didn't find the rooster," she said. "Will you help me look?"

"Of course I will." He started flipping pages. "I'll find the one in the book, and you . . . " He whispered the rest into her ear. "Look out the window and find the real rooster out there."

"Stop whispering. Put down the book," the rich man said. "I'm waiting for the answer to my question: Who stole my money? Tell me!"

Crayfish flipped on. "I'm sorry, Sir, but I must find the page I'm looking for in this all-knowing book of mine."

The rich man rapped his knuckles on the table. He didn't notice—Crayfish and Maggie didn't either—that the cook slipped ever so quietly in from the kitchen, and crept into the stove (it wasn't lit), so he could eavesdrop on what the doctor would say.

Crayfish kept leafing through the book, not finding the rooster, and muttered,

"I know you're in there. You'd better come out!"

He means me,

thought the cook in

the stove, and got

so frightened, he j u m p e d out

and dashed from the room.

"The *cook* stole my money?" yelled the rich man, thumping on the table.

"Papa, Papa, I see the rooster!" Maggie shouted. She was looking out the window, past the fishpond, past the flower garden, to the chicken coop, which she could glimpse by leaning sideways in her chair. "I found the real rooster! He's over there!"

"Yes, there he is!" Crayfish smiled. He gave Maggie a kiss.

Then he asked the rich man, "Sir, will you kindly come with us?"

The rich man said, "Not till you answer my question."

"Do come. You won't regret it, Sir," said Crayfish very nicely.

"Oh, very well." The rich man changed his mind and went along.

And Maggie led the way, she knew just where to go—

around the fishpond,

through the flower garden,

over to the chicken coop—

The rooster stood atop the roof and crowed, "Kee-ker-ree-kee-kee!"

"Why have you brought me here?" the rich man asked.

Crayfish said, "Come in, you'll see."

The door was low. They had to

crouch to enter.

"Look around, Sir," Crayfish said.

The rich man looked all around, he dug

into a pile of straw—and whooped with joy.

"My money!" He scooped up golden coins galore.

"You *knew* where it was! I thank you, dear Doctor All-Knowing!"

Then he asked, "*Now* will you tell who stole it?"

Do you suppose the "doctor" told?

No, he didn't.

The servants rewarded him well. So did the rich man. Now Crayfish
was no longer poor, and very happy. So was Maggie. And they never went
hungry anymore. They had good suppers with many courses, and always
delicious dessert: cake, or pie, or pudding—and sometimes all three!—at

the end

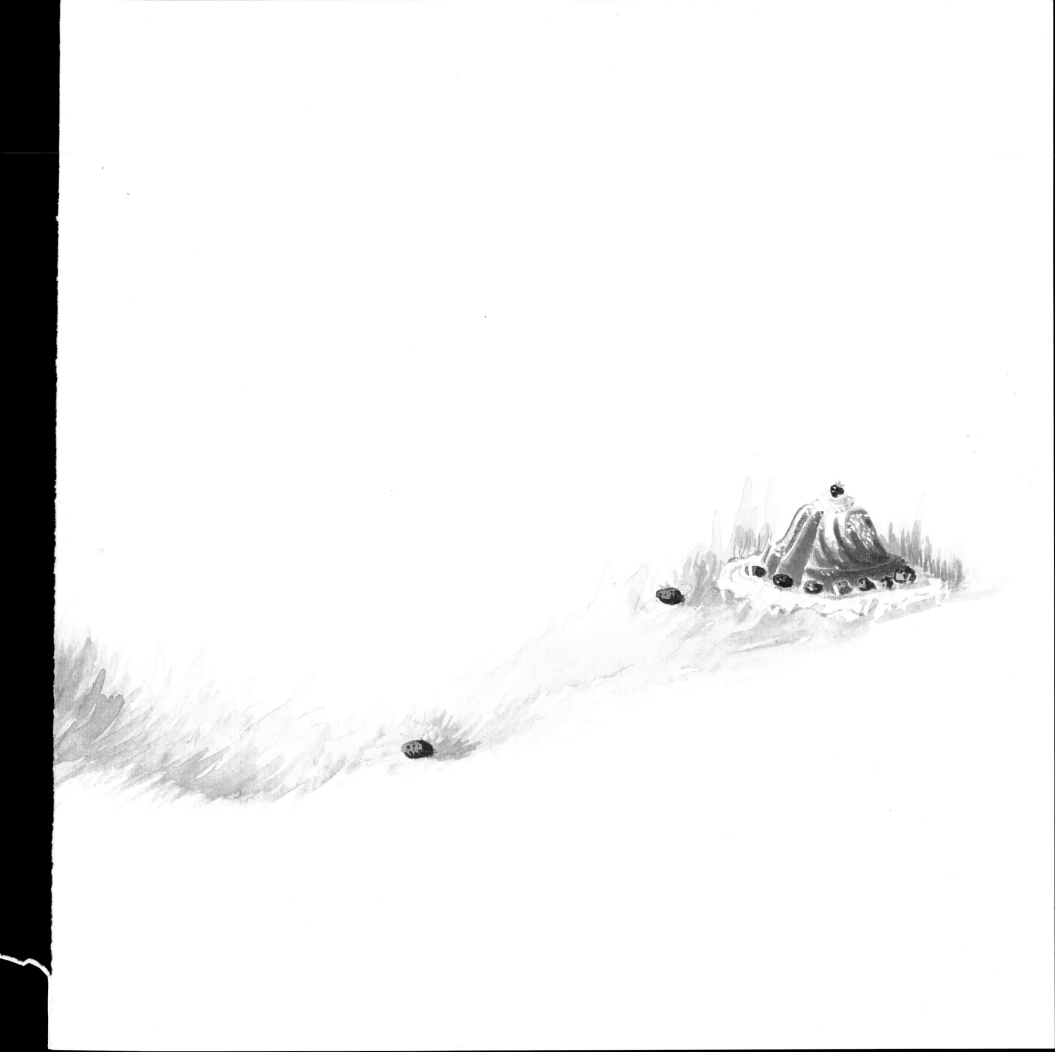